GO AWAY, UNICORN!

For my sisters Leigh-Anne and Lindsay

Scholastic Children's Books,
Euston House,
24 Eversholt Street,
London NW1 1DB, UK
A division of Scholastic Ltd

London ~ New York ~ Toronto ~ Sydney ~ Auckland
Mexico City ~ New Delhi ~ Hong Kong

First published in Canada by McKellar & Martin Publishing Group Ltd, 2010

Published in the US by Scholastic Inc., 2019
This edition published in the UK by Scholastic Ltd, 2019
Text and illustrations © Emily Mullock, 2010
ISBN 978 1407 19689 3

Printed and bound in Italy by L.E.G.O S.p.A

2 4 6 8 10 9 7 5 3 1

www.scholastic.co.uk

GO AWAY, UNICORN!

Text & illustrations by

EMILY MULLOCK

SCHOLASTIC

Alice met the unicorn at her tenth birthday party in the park.

He had not been invited.

The unicorn had come because he'd smelled cake (his *most* favourite food).

He stayed because he'd seen Alice.

Now, you have to be pretty silly to think that Alice was a unicorn just because of her shiny, gold party hat.

But unicorns can be pretty silly.

Her friend Patty said, "You got a unicorn for your birthday??!! All I got was a boring goldfish."

Alice shrugged. She had no use for a unicorn.

Even so, the unicorn played party games, he gave rides on his back and he let everyone pet his luxurious, sparkly mane.

But when the party was over, and everyone had gone home, the unicorn was still there.

Alice said,

"GO AWAY, UNICORN."

But unicorns aren't very good listeners.

Alice was not pleased that the unicorn had
followed her home. "This is silly," she said, and
took off her party hat. "See? I'm not some weird
horse. I can't be your friend."

Alice frowned. She said,

"GO AWAY, UNICORN."

But unicorns know a friend
when they see one.
So, the unicorn moved in.

He made a nest for himself in her bedroom. He
used pages from Alice's favourite books and some
old, shiny wrapping paper.
He was very comfortable.

He ate her cereal – but only the tiny,
pink marshmallows, which were, of course, the
best part.

He used all of her shampoo
to wash his mane . . .

. . . Alice said,

"GO AWAY, UNICORN."

But unicorns are easily distracted.
The unicorn hogged the remote.
He trod glitter through the house.
He snored all night.
And he followed Alice to school.

. . . Alice said,

"GO AWAY, UNICORN."

But unicorns can be very sneaky.

Alice's teacher asked,
"Where is your homework?"
"My unicorn ate it," Alice replied.

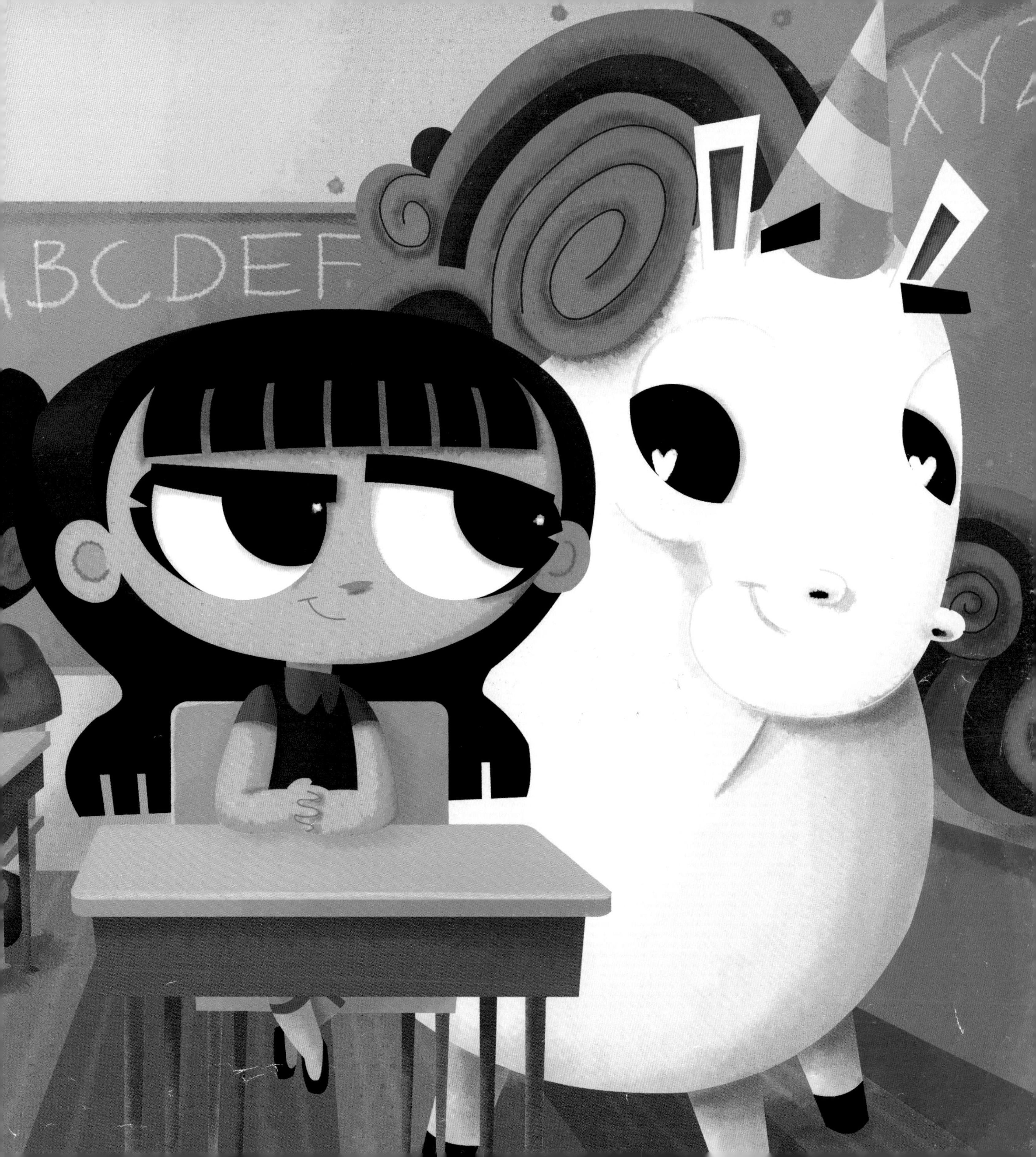
BCDEF

That unicorn just would not go.

Alice tried to tell him he was a mythical creature. "That means you don't exist," she explained.

But that just made the unicorn feel more special.

She tried to lose him in the park, but he just thought it was a game.

She tried to ship him to the zoo, but the zookeeper said, "I'm sorry. Unicorns don't exist."

"I know that!" Alice cried, and buried her head in her hands.

The unicorn could tell something was wrong.

It's a good thing unicorns know just how to cheer up a friend.

The unicorn turned Alice's hair bright pink. Pink was his *most* favourite colour.

Pink made Alice want to throw up.

Alice had had enough.

She stared at her hair.
She stared at the unicorn.

She said the meanest thing
she could think of:

"You are *so* not my friend.
I would rather have a goldfish than you!"

Even unicorns know when
they're being insulted.
So the unicorn left.
And he did not come back.

It was very quiet with no snoring.

And it was very dull with no glitter.

And it was very plain in Alice's house with no pink.

But most of all, it was very lonely with no best friend.

Alice might not have known a lot about being best friends, but she was pretty sure that the unicorn was doing a lot better job of it than she was.

Alice whispered,

"COME BACK, UNICORN."

Unicorns have very good hearing.

Alice hugged her unicorn. She said, "Sometimes even best friends fight."

Unicorns know an apology when they hear one.

HAPPY BIRTHDAY, ALICE!